This edition published by Parragon Books Ltd in 2014

Parragon Books Ltd
Chartist House
15–17 Trim Street
Bath BA1 1HA, UK
www.parragon.com

ISBN 978-1-4723-5887-5

Printed in China

PaRragon

Bath • New York • Cologne • Melbourne • Delhi
Hong Kong • Shenzhen • Singapore • Amsterdam

Three years had passed since Dusty had won
the Wings Around The Globe Rally and he had been
unstoppable ever since.

When Dusty wasn't racing, he spent his time in
Propwash Junction, where everyone was preparing for
the annual Corn Festival.

Dusty grinned. "It's gonna be the
biggest Corn Fest yet!"

One day, Skipper, Dusty's coach, was pushing the champ hard in a training run. Suddenly, Dusty's engine stuttered and he fell into a spin!

"Dusty? Dusty? What's wrong?" Skipper asked worriedly.

Dusty couldn't answer because he was out of breath and felt sick. Dusty began to lose altitude.

"Whoa, steady there," hollered Skipper.

Luckily, Dusty regained control and Skipper helped him land safely.

Dottie, Dusty's mechanic, had bad news. "Your gearbox is failing," she told him. Even worse, it couldn't be replaced because it was out of production.

Dottie fitted Dusty with a warning gauge. "If the light comes on, you need to slow down," she said. "I'm so sorry."

Later in the evening, Dusty wanted to prove he could still be a racer. He took off into the night sky and sped across the treetops.

Suddenly, the warning light flashed. As Dusty slowed down, he looked ahead to see that he was too close to a tall tower. He clipped the top of it, landed hard and skidded right into the airport's petrol station!

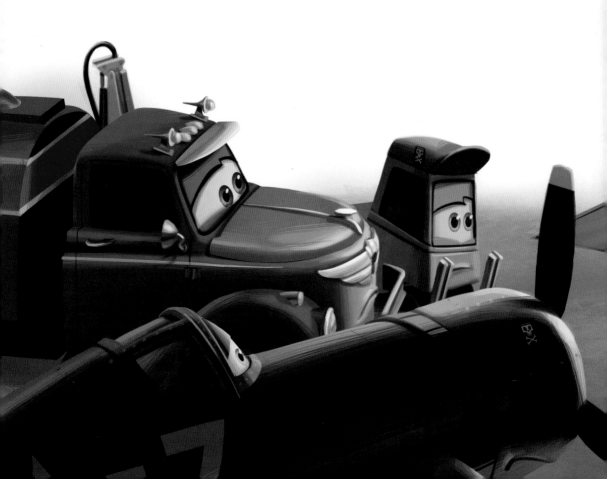

The petrol station's roof collapsed and a petrol pump exploded. KABOOM!

Mayday, the airport's fire engine, tried to put out the fire but his leaky old fire hose was no good. Desperate, he called for volunteers to help topple a water tower.

Mayday, Skipper, Chug and Dusty pulled down the tower together and the water put out the fire.

The next day, two safety officials declared that Propwash Junction's airport would be shut down until Mayday was upgraded and a second certified firefighter was hired. The Corn Festival would have to be cancelled!

Dusty felt bad about the fire and wanted to find a way to help. Then he realized he could be Propwash's new firefighter!

The next day, Dusty flew off towards the air attack base in Piston Peak National Park. Mayday's friend Blade Ranger, the head of the base, had agreed to train Dusty.

Dusty arrived just in time to see Dipper, Cabbie, Windlifter and the smokejumpers spring into action as they were called to a fire.

Blade, a rescue copter, was already on the scene. Dusty watched as he dumped fire retardant onto the blaze. Everyone worked together to put the fire out.

Back at the base, Dusty explained he was there to be trained as a firefighter. Maru, the mechanic, replaced Dusty's landing gear with pontoons. "I rebuilt these," he said proudly. "They're better than new."

Dusty's training started at Anchor Lake with lessons on how to fill his pontoons with water. Then Blade tested Dusty's low-altitude flying at Augerin Canyon – Dusty aced the course.

During the training Dusty's warning light flashed on and made him back off.

"If you don't push it," Blade warned, "you won't be certified."

The next day, Dusty practised putting out flaming barrels. After trying again and again, hitting one target was the best he could do.

Dusty headed back to the hangar, discouraged. But Skipper, Chug and Dottie radioed him with some good news – they had found him a new gearbox!

"Wow, thanks! That's the best news," replied Dusty. He couldn't have been happier.

Just then, the Park Superintendent, Cad Spinner, arrived. When Cad realized Dusty was the famous racer he excitedly invited him to the grand reopening of his lodge.

But Blade was worried because he knew that Cad had packed too many visitors into the lodge before, which was a fire risk.

After a hard day fighting a large fire, Dusty, Dipper, Windlifter and Maru arrived at the lodge reopening party.

Dusty met Harvey and Winnie, a couple celebrating their 50th wedding anniversary. They were trying to find the spot where they first kissed. Harvey described that it was near a waterfall....

"That sounds like Augerin Canyon," said Dusty, helpfully.

Dusty hung out with his new firefighter friends at the party. They told him they all had jobs before they started fighting fires. Dusty realized that a life without racing might not be so bad.

The next morning, Dusty received some disappointing news from back home. The gearbox had arrived, but it was the wrong one.

Dusty couldn't believe it. His racing days were over.

Moments later, Dusty and the firefighters were called to action – there were two new wildfires.

The fires were moving towards the lodge. Maru radioed the lodge and told Cad to get everyone out, but Cad refused. He wasn't about to let a little fire spoil his celebration.

After the news from home, Dusty was distracted and didn't pay attention to Blade's orders, so Blade told him to return to base.

Instead, Dusty flew down to the lake to reload his pontoons. But his nose hit the water and his engine stalled. Not able to fly, Dusty drifted over the waterfall. Blade swooped in, threw a line to Dusty and swung him to safety.

On the ground, Dusty confessed that he had to give up racing.

Blade sighed. "Life doesn't always go the way you expect it. But you came here to become a firefighter, so don't give up."

But there was no time to rest. The fire was closing in fast! They took shelter inside an old mine and Blade used his body to shield Dusty from the heat.

When the fire had burned past, the two slowly emerged. Blade was badly damaged and crashed as he tried to take off. Dusty radioed the base for help.

Meanwhile, the fire closed in on
the lodge and everyone was evacuated.
But as they tried to leave, their path was
blocked by a burning tree.

Back at base, Windlifter took command as Blade recovered
and the firefighters put out the fires that surrounded the guests.

But not everyone had escaped. Harvey and Winnie were
trapped on a burning bridge in Augerin Canyon.

Dusty flew to the waterfall to fill his pontoons. He had to
push hard as he pulled straight up and skimmed the face of
the waterfall. The warning light flashed red.

Dusty managed to drop the water on the flames and
save his friends, but his engine cut out and he
crashed into the forest.

Days later, Dusty, still groggy, rolled out of Maru's hangar. His firefighting friends were there to greet him.

Maru had good news for Dusty. Not only had he patched up Dusty on the outside, he had used spare parts to build him a custom-made gearbox!

"I'd say you earned that certification," said Blade.

Dusty cranked the engine and his propeller sprang to life!

"Better than new," said Maru.

Dusty was glad to be home. While he was away, Dottie had completely updated Mayday. Now that Propwash had two certified firefighters, it was open for business again.

The Corn Festival got into full swing.

"Ladies and gentleplanes, the Corn Fest is proud to present the Piston Peak Air Attack Team and our very own Dusty Crophopper!" announced Chug.

Everyone cheered as the firefighters flew by. Then Dusty, with his engine pushed to the max, came in low and soaked every target.

BULLSEYE!